BIPOLAR
COWBOY

Also by Noah Cicero

Go to work and do your job. Care for your children. Pay your bills. Obey the law. Buy products.

The Collected Works of Noah Cicero Vol. 1

The Collected Works of Noah Cicero Vol. 2

The Noah Cicero Bathroom Reader

BIPOLAR COWBOY
Noah Cicero

LAZY FASCIST PRESS

LAZY FASCIST PRESS
PO Box 10065
Portland, OR 97296

www.lazyfascistpress.com

ISBN: 978-1-62105-178-7

Printed in the USA.

CONTENTS

This book of love poems is for all those
who loved so deeply
it crossed the line
into mental illness

Chronology of the
Bipolar Cowboy Dream

June 2011: Noah Cicero and Jordan Castro fly from Ohio to LA to film the movie *Shoplifting from American Apparel*. Jordan and Noah are on Adderall the entire time. Bebe Zeva shows up and smokes a few cigarettes.

August 2011: Stevie Nicks and Noah Cicero drive a car to Santa Fe, New Mexico. The cicadas scare Stevie Nicks. They go to the Palace of the Governors, the oldest building in America. Apaches sell expensive goods on the street. Stevie Nicks and Noah Cicero paint a giant picture one night.

March 2012: Stevie Nicks and Noah Cicero go to Japan to teach ESL for one year.

December 2012: Stevie Nicks and Noah Cicero go to Cambodia for one week. See Angkor Wat. There seems to be magic there, but their western minds have a hard time trying to understand it.

March 2013: Noah Cicero leaves Japan, goes back to America.

April 2013: Noah Cicero's mentor, an old bluegrass guitarist from Kentucky, dies from lung cancer. The old man, a few years earlier on Christmas, gave him a black Martin guitar. Noah Cicero brings the guitar with him everywhere.

April 2013: Stevie Nicks leaves this reality and goes to an alternate Murakami-based reality with two moons.

May 2013: Noah Cicero flies to the Grand Canyon. At the Grand Canyon he hikes 90 miles. He sits among the desert pinyons and watches families of javelinas walk by. He meets an old Navajo woman. She teaches him a few words of Navajo.

September 2013: Goes to Las Vegas for two weeks, then flies back to Ohio for two weeks. Stays at his parents' house. He rides a bicycle around the old neighborhood. Noah Cicero and his friend Bernice, a 31-year-old woman who is a nurse and basically takes care of Noah Cicero, drive a 64-year-old woman, a 15-year-old boy named James, and two cats across America to Las Vegas in a rented Chrysler minivan.

October 2013: Noah Cicero lives in Las Vegas, cannot find a job.

October 2013: Chiungyi visits Las Vegas for 12 days. They go to Zion National Park.

November 2013: Noah Cicero's friend Nicky visits from Santa Fe, New Mexico. They go to Valley of Fire State Park.

December 2013: Noah Cicero still has no job. He drinks every night listening to sad songs by George Jones on his adobe porch.

No matter how much he drinks he can't forget her.

January 2014: Noah Cicero and Bernice visit Death Valley. They walk into the Ubehebe where humans came from Coyote's basket.

January 2014: Noah Cicero moves to Scotts Mills, Oregon to live in an A-frame house in the forest on an old logging road. He spends most of his days alone walking the forest with a yellow labrador named Fin. He spends the days reading Bodhidharma and Chuang Tzu.

March 2014: Noah Cicero moves to Portland, Oregon for several weeks before suffering a total nervous breakdown and driving back to Las Vegas.

March 2014: Returns to Las Vegas. Seeks medical help, gets on medication.

April 2014: There are no more transmissions from Stevie Nicks from the world of two moons. Noah Cicero tells himself she was eaten by an unknown creature living in the world of two moons.

April/May 2014: Noah Cicero writes this book of poetry.

July 2014: Noah Cicero lives in Las Vegas, feels peaceful. He has direction, not a goal but a direction. He has a job and friends and he feels okay. Bebe Zeva somehow shows up at the end. Noah Cicero gives her this amazing shirt he bought in Cambodia.

NOTE 1

This book of love poems says nothing
about *la condition humaine.*

It is intimate.

Do not try to look for life answers
in this book of love poems.

The universals are not here.

Only the personals.

NOTE 2

This book of poems
is merely a moment, a feeling.
That came from Noah Cicero in April/May 2014.
By the time this book comes out,
the Noah Cicero who wrote this book,
won't exist.

Noah Cicero hopes this book will change him.

Moon Head

"How did the moon
get into your head?"

"Why did you try to stick
the earth
in your head, did you
need it all?"

Eating Alone

After his girlfriend left,
she told him
it was over
during a car ride
to his parents' house. He doesn't
even remember what she said—

He felt so shocked by it,
he didn't even notice. He
just consented—

Now he makes two scrambled eggs
instead of four.
Now he doesn't order pizza.

Theology

This isn't an argument,
I don't want to win or lose
on ObamaCare or who caused
the relationship to fail,
of if mom you really loved me.

I am going to walk
to the gas station,
and on the way there, I'm going
to pick a leaf off a tree,
and play with it,
in my fingers.

Proof of God

I was in Oregon,
and saw a place
called Best Teriyaki.

It seemed odd,
so fucking unbelievable,
that white people came and killed
all the buffalo, wiped out or moved
into tiny spaces all the Chinook people.

Then a guy or woman from Japan, from
a country doing great in terms of development,
decided to come to Oregon, a forest where the sun
hardly ever shines, where it rains rains rains and
every white man has a beard, even if it makes him
less handsome.
And the Japanese person opens a business that has the
Best Teriyaki on the Planet Earth.

The very concept, the idea, the notion,
the phenomenological existence of

Best Teriyaki proved to me that the universe
was truly weird, that anything could happen,
because if the Best Teriyaki could be located
inside a forest on the western edge of North America,
anything could be possible.

A Way Somehow

I don't know, at times,
if you are really people, I
know you are people, I mean,
you aren't walking on fours, and you
wear clothes. (But sometimes, when
you're naked, I don't know if you are human,
and get confused, that's why I don't
go to strip joints anymore, or have sex.)

How did you all become people? How did
you get so good at showing up on time for work,
and doing what your manager says, how did you
get so good at being detailed-oriented. There
is an ad on Craigslist for a processor, that says, "*We are
looking for someone seriously ready to start a career
and care about the work they do every day.*"
Seriously the ad doesn't even state what the
company produces? How the fuck can you people
care about some unknown something, will you even care
after you get the job?

How do you become a person?
Usually, instead of trying to get a job,
I listen to music on YouTube, instead of being
a person, I try to become the notes of songs,
the chord structure of "Will You Still Love Me Tomorrow"
covered by Amy Winehouse, I want to become that song, I learn
the song on guitar and strum it on my adobe porch thing,
trying to become non-human, sometimes I try to become
the taste of a Carl's Jr. cheeseburger, I want to be
that delicious, that bad for you.

Sometimes I listen to Amitabha chants,
Navajo chants, even old
Kentucky Old Regular Baptists call out chants, I
want to be a pure feeling, that may lead to heaven,
but instead I am Noah Cicero, sometimes I scream, I
can't be controlled, I can't be tamed, because I
don't know what to be—

When you see a pronghorn antelope from your car, high up
north in Nevada, by the Walker River Rez. I don't know
what to be, the antelope, the person seeing the antelope, the grass
that the antelope is eating, the feeling the person gets from
seeing the antelope, the feeling the antelope has while
eating the grass, so I try to be all things, then I realize,
I'm just wind, swirling and swirling, and it is okay, and
it isn't okay,
and all will work itself out, something is taking its course, but
it never works out, and all all all it comes, and the wind
shaking the leaves of the palm tree, the hum of bugs, and
me trying to find a job on Craigslist.

Say it to me Now

I sent her an email,
it said, "Call at 8pm, your time
today, and read these sentences
to me, don't even wait for me to say
hello, just start reading—

Noah, you will never see me again.
Noah, you will never hold me again.
Noah, if we are in the same room, we cannot
kiss, we cannot touch, we cannot do
anything physical together, because
I have a new boyfriend.

At night or when I'm bored at work, I will
remember sitting with you
next to the Cuyahoga and Meguro River.
I will even remember the
river in Santa Fe that had no water."

Then in a peaceful voice, say—
"Goodbye Noah."

She never called that day. He received
an email four days later stating, "Noah,
get it together, it's been a year. Watch
some Greta Gerwig movies, and get
over it."

Valley of Fire

Sometimes I lie down
in the desert,
trying to become
as quiet as a cactus

sometimes I wish
I could become
a cactus

My favorite cactus is the
escobaria vivipara—
It is funny, it is shaped
like a beehive.

One People Named Randy

This planet has a lot of people
on it.
I've seen people in Ohio, Canada,
New York City, on the edge of the Grand Canyon,
down in Baja, in Japan and Cambodia, I saw them,
with their faces, hands, everyone
has a different face, everyone has a different
opinion on heaven, and their opinions and
their faces are vital to their identity, to their beauty,
to their song.

We all seem to have the same universal
urgencies.
Love, family, dealing with change,
missing people. Maybe we
are all one person named Randy.

And Randy is super bipolar, and
maybe even a cutter.

Lo Siento

I am sorry—
to the girl in Poland,
to the girl in Seattle,
to the mail order bride from the Philippines.
And even to the stalker Romanian girl—
I cannot love you—
you seem really nice,
even a little funny.

But my heart, my brain,
even my penis still protests,
for another, still plays the old songs.

Maybe one day, when I'm
not paying attention, someone
will slip into my heart, just imagined
my heart in the desert, maybe Death Valley.
Where the dunes are, a rattlesnake comes upon
my heart, biting it and
pouring venom into it.

Coyote

1.

In the Grand Canyon
employee dining room.
A 72-year-old Navajo woman
worked cleaning tables.

The government made her
go to Cleveland for school, so she
became friends with Noah from
the Cleveland area
who worked the register.

She was from Steamboat,
on the Navajo Rez.

She had her name
tattooed on her hand.
She said she did it
when she was 14
with a cactus needle,

the ultimate stick and poke.

Noah Cicero would talk to her
about Navajo/Hopi/Zuni religion.

The God of the Navajos is Changing Woman,
who made love to the sun,
that created the son who killed the monsters.

And Coyote runs around the western lands
doing tricks on humans to show them
that they are taking life too serious.

One day Noah mentioned Changing Woman,
and the old Navajo woman said,
"Don't mention my religion, you don't believe,"
in a forceful voice.

Noah felt really bad. Not only because
he hurt her feelings, but because
he knew he believed in nothing.

The funny thing was, he didn't know
why he didn't believe in anything.

2.

Noah Cicero's friend Nicky
came to Las Vegas.

Grew up together in Ohio,
both exiled.

He to New Mexico,
Noah to Nevada.

To the desert.

They did the tourist things,
went to Valley of Fire
in the twilight.

They walked among the 3,000-year-old petroglyphs,
done by a people long dead. (No one has any
idea who drew them, Noah liked the idea of pictures
without ideas.)

Little drawings of animals and families.

Families that looked like aliens?
Kind of?

Nicky and Noah walked off the trail,
they sat on a red cliff,
talking about vision quests
and grad programs.

Nicky who doesn't hike much,
wanted to hike around a certain red rock,
assuming it would return to the trail.

But they were lost, with the sun setting,
no water, no food, lost among giant red rocks,
basically Mars.

Nicky thought it was fun, but the sun was setting,
it was getting colder and colder.
Noah who had hiked 150 miles in the desert,
knew they would get sick without water,
get really cold, and there would be zero light
in a place called Valley of Fire.

Noah stopped Nicky.
"Nicky, if we get trapped out here,
no water, it is 58 degrees but in
four hours it will be 33. No light,
no food, our lives just got
very serious."

Nicky's facial expression changed.
He understood.

They kept walking, scrambling,
but ending up nowhere.

The sun setting darkness coming.

With Nicky ahead,
Noah Cicero put his hands together
and prayed. Not to anything specific,
just a good old-fashioned
"save our asses" prayer.

They walked and scrambled,
Noah kept looking for tracks
in the sand, but the footprints
would disappear when they hit
the red rocks. He found some
small paw prints
and followed them.

With barely any light left,
they found the road.

When they got back to the car,
a coyote walked out of the brush,
strolled past them, and went back
into the desert.

3.

At the Rhyolite ghost town,
deep in the Nevada desert,
60 miles north
of Las Vegas.

Nothing but Joshua trees and lizards.

Noah Cicero walks among the ruins.
A couple, man and woman, sit on a bench.
Noah says, "Hi, where are you from?"
They respond, "Vienna, Ohio."

Noah's hometown.

There are over 30,000 towns
in the United States. And they
were the only other American tourists there.

Noah walked away laughing,
"Coyote and his tricks."

And he meant it.

George Jones

I went to the library on West Charleston,
by the community college.
I looked at the community college, and
considered taking a class on Excel
and Quickbooks.

Went into the library and returned
Pearl Jam's greatest hits. I'm
on mood stabilizers, and I just took
an anti-anxiety pill. Recently,
I've been crying, having panic attacks.

I am high in the West Charleston Library.
Nobody in the library knows how lonely
I am. I thank them for that.

Go over to the CDs, stand in
front of the country CDs, I can
barely move, time doesn't exist
on these pills. I see George Jones,
he is like my brother. I hold the

George Jones CD, he has a buzzcut,
the songs are from his early career.
I say, "George Jones,
you are my brother. My real brother
is a douchebag who won't talk to me,
but George Jones you have
never rejected me. You are like
my Jesus, I knock and you let me in."

I walk over to the religion section, and
find a book on Taoism that I never heard of. I am
holding *Yuan Dao: Tracing Dao to
Its Source*. I am going to listen to George Jones
and then trace the Dao, I have—
become a real freak.

Could I get any weirder? God?
Did you know that George Jones
has a cover of "I'll Fly Away" and
it ain't that bad.

A Three-Pronged Tree

There is a Douglas fir, on an
old logging road in Scotts Mills, Oregon.
It is three-pronged—
when it was little, it was struck by lightning, in
a horrible moment of agony. The tree
became three-pronged. It became
a deformed version of its species.

Years later lumberjacks came to
cut the forest down, they looked
at the deformed tree, and were
amazed.

I like to imagine the lumberjacks
standing looking at the
three-pronged tree, big guys
with strong muscles and slightly
flabby bellies, sweaty, wearing baseball caps.
Men nothing like me, but in a way,
exactly like me.

The boss stares at it and says,
"I like it, a three-pronged Douglas fir, you
don't see that every day. I think we
should leave it."

The lumberjacks let it remain.

It remains there, surrounded by new growth, and
people still walk by and stop to look at
the deformed plant. In America we
don't have shrines of monks or saints or
magic rivers to gather by and swim in, in America
we leave three-pronged Douglas firs to
worship at and give praise. We take
a picture with our iPhone, send it to our friends,
and call it love.

That Mazzy Star Song

Standing on Foster Road in Southeast Portland,
drizzle drizzle drizzle
the sky, the earth a big shadow.

Noah stood on the street,
looked around and thought
"This looks like fucking Ohio."

He began crying, hyperventilating.
He just wanted it to be over.

He moved into a small room,
in some weird guy's apartment. The weird guy said
he loved art. He used the word
'bohemian.'

The man had two cats, they didn't
seem evil when Noah first met them.

In the middle of the night, the cats
scratched on the door. Noah heard

the scratching, quick memory burst—
not good, of 2011. When he first met her.
Sleeping in her room in Oberlin, Ohio.
Her roommate's cat, Tuna, would always
scratch on her door at night. Tuna would
stick his little paw under the door.
Noah liked looking down at the cat paw.

But now,
the cat scratching the door, there was a
horrible, tumultuous noise inside his head.

He woke up the next morning in hell, a violent hell
that involved Noah Cicero killing himself
on repeat.

Noah Cicero stood on Foster Road
in Southeast Portland.

Isn't Portland supposed to be heaven?
Where did these evil cats come from?

Noah packed up his clothes
and Buddhist beads, got into
a car and started driving back to Las Vegas.

He drove through the Cascades,
through the cold desert. He had only one CD.
It was a mix CD his friend made.
The only good song on it was
that Mazzy Star song
"Fade Into You."

Noah listened to that song on repeat.
He remembered his brother Michael,
long dead of a gunshot to the head,
in Kentucky.
His brother liked that Mazzy Star song.
Noah remembered that Michael
ordered 16 CDs from BMG for one penny.

Noah could see
some of the CDs in his mind,
floating around—
Elton John's *Greatest Hits*, 4 Non Blondes,
Rod Stewart, Eddie Money, Violent Femmes,
and that Mazzy Star album.

Noah wanted to find Mazzy Star, he wondered
if they had become bipolar cowboys.

The Last Phone Call

She started texting, while
I was at Vons on Lake Mead.
I had stopped texting and sending emails,
didn't know what to say.
But I've been feeling better lately, the pills
are causing smoother neural connections.
(The old Noah
is slowly returning. But not quite there.)

I called her in the Vons parking lot. She sounded
nice, she kept laughing,
(her laughter felt like heaven to him, he could
hear the heaven in her giggles)
and she let me
talk a lot. (He has been talking so much lately, just words
and words, come and come.)
She let me speak so many words. There was
no fighting
no condescending remarks
no blaming.
A new peace had come, laughter had come,

She hated being embarrassed.
A proud Italian-Catholic girl, she takes the male role,
never lets her emotions become untamed.

She told him how she saw an old friend
in front of a coffee shop, Lake Erie a ten minute
walk away, the icy waves crashing, snow on the
branches,
snow pushed into high piles, winter coats,
big hats covering ears.
She saw an old flame from five years smoking, she said
her big sunglasses were on, and hoped
he did not see her, she couldn't walk alone
the streets of Cleveland, too many chances
for embarrassment.

She told me her new boy was wholesome. She said,
"You are not wholesome."

It is true, I am not wholesome.

I could hear her voice grow weak, I wasn't talking
of serious things, just talking, but her voice,
it became delicate, like she was choking, she could
only answer yes or no, then it hit me,
she was crying.

And she was trying hard to make sure I didn't notice.

I saw her face, in her bedroom, in Cleveland, Ohio.

She didn't like crying, such a weak expression,
she felt
embarrassed.

We got off the phone soon after,

I sent her a text
"One day you'll embarrass yourself
in front of me
and it will be the greatest day of your life."

She never texted back. I imagined she smiled,
then went to the bathroom and cried, maybe looked
in the mirror and felt the
hard hard
confusion.

The hard hard
"how"

(She actually rolled her eyes and went back to texting her new
boy.)

NOTE

Noah Cicero is suffering from mental illness, he recently had a nervous breakdown. He reads into everything, he overthinks everything, he comes up with ten truths. Strangely one of the ten truths he comes up with is actually true. But sadly, life never lets us know what the absolute truth ever is.

Life gives us many truths and we have to pick one.

The math of building a bridge is usually always true. We do the calculations and if the bridge holds cars and gets humans across rivers, the math is true. But should we build the bridge, where should we put the bridge, how often should we maintain the bridge, when will we no longer require the bridge? We never know for sure.

If we knew the absolute truth, would things change?

Are we looking for the absolute truth or the absolute feeling? Or the answer that best suits our personal needs?

When it comes to love, there is no Occam's razor, love is ineffable.

Noah believed and often said, "You can't choose who you love."

Noah didn't know if that was a religious or a scientific philosophy.

He rationalized it in two ways—

1. The Science Way

Love came from the inner darkness. Somewhere deep in the childhood of every person were these moments, these obsessions, the training of one's parents on how to love, on what to love, and it was so deep, it was like a song.

Noah believed everyone was like a song. Everyone is playing a song all the time, and when we find someone who plays a song like our song, then we become friends, and if the song is close enough, then we become lovers, even if it is only for a night.

Noah believed it was like music, because there is no getting to the bottom of a song, millions of people can create opinions on a single song for a million years, but the beauty of a song can't ever be reached, it always remains different for everyone—

People are like that, songs. Everyone has a slightly different reaction to every other person they meet.

Noah believed that the reasons people loved each other, if said out loud, were often scary, because the answers for love often included balance, and often in humans the worst and best of us go into balance. Often one is a little lazy and the other a little busy, one is a little selfish and the other a little selfless, one a little unstable and the other stable—

But there is no need to say what the dark things are, most never do, and the world goes on.

2. The Mystical Way

According to Aristophanes, before the beginning—

There were creatures with two heads. They walked around having two heads, sometimes the two heads fought, sometimes the two were friendly, but they had to work together to stay alive and be two-headed people.

The two were linked, something deep, from the beginning—

According to the Navajos, we all come from when Changing Woman had sex with the sun and gave birth to humankind.

We all have light in us.

The two-headed creatures had light.

According to Christians, "*1. In the beginning was the Word, and the Word was with God, and the Word was God. 2. He was with God in the beginning. 3. Through him all things were made; without him nothing was made that has been made. 4. In him was life, and that life was the light of all mankind. 5. The light shines in the darkness, and the darkness has not overcome it.*"

Noah considered this one of the most beautiful things he had ever read. His favorite part, the thing that made him weep, was "*and the darkness has not overcome it.*"

Noah believed that there were lights inside people. He even believed that there were lights inside animals, inside mountains, inside plants, inside trees, Noah went so far to believe that there was even light in interactions, that there was light everywhere. That it made sense that Changing Woman had sex with the sun, because there was so much light.

But how does all this relate back to Aristophanes and his two-headed creatures.

All of the two-headed creatures had a light inside them, and the light had a very specific color and crackle, because the light burned from the same wood, from the same incense.

And humans are reincarnated many times over, finding that other creature over and over again—but Noah also believed there were families of souls born over and over again, destined to meet in every life or at least in a high ratio of them. And we know somehow, as soon as we meet, that we are old friends, that there is some infinite song, always playing.

Sometimes Noah felt like screaming, "Do you hear my song? Does anyone hear my song?"

Noah believed he had found his other head. But he was on

medication. Prior to a few years ago, Noah was a normal atheist, living his George Carlin/Richard Dawkins life. He read Sartre and was a sophisticated man.

But he watched a man die, and visited Angkor Wat, and the mandala of his mind had been destroyed.

Now he had rocks under his pillow to keep bad dreams away and a wooden Buddha he prayed to every morning.

Noah recently saw a movie called *Buddha Avalokiteshvara,* made in China. Noah has no idea how to say 'Avalokiteshvara' out loud.

In the movie a Japanese monk wants a mystic green statue of Buddha Avalokiteshvara to bring back to Japan, to make peace in Japan.

To get this statue, the monk sits for a week on his knees praying and reciting sutras, with no food, no water, nothing. Eventually the Chinese monk gives him the mystic green statue, because he shows his sincerity.

Noah didn't know if he was a desperado who was sincerely in love with a woman, and because his love was so strong, so sincere, that he had to bumble about the west like a cowboy, waiting for the day when she said, "Come home."

That work didn't matter, money didn't matter, how the world looked at him did not matter, if he was the richest man, or the poorest man, it did not matter. The only thing that mattered was his sincerity of love.

But it might not be sincerity.

It might be total and awesome genetic mental illness!

All of it, every last idea he had concerning this woman, his reality, the world around him, was a construction of his agony to deal with a reality he found to be intolerable.

Then Noah Cicero stared out the window of Starbucks and thought, "But doesn't Buddha want me to let go of all attachment? Shouldn't I just let her go? Monks aren't even allowed to touch women."

But Noah wasn't raised in a Buddhist country, he didn't grow up in a culture that would cultivate the personality traits that would blossom in a monastery, he grew up in America, a white guy with blue eyes. Enlightenment for a white man was marriage, kids, and then finding peace and wisdom in living a hard-working responsible life. Shit, when Sartre, who was supposed to be beyond all conventions, picked a personality trait we should all focus on, it was responsibility, the white man's favorite goal, responsibility.

Noah Cicero sat in a wooden chair holding a Starbucks cup, half-filled with coffee. He stared at his shoes. Everyone that loves him stood in front of him, everyone that truly cares about him, they said in chorus, "Addiction is selfish. You are addicted to this person, while we are all here, we love your jokes, we love your thoughts, we love to go to parks and hike and drink beer with you too. Are we not good enough? We are tired of hearing about her, we are tired of you being sad. She makes you sad she makes you sad she makes you sad she makes you sad she makes you sad. And we can't watch it anymore."

But what the people who loved Noah could not understand was that he thought his addiction was sincerity, that he loved the uncertainty of the whole event. The mixture of Buddhist/Taoist ideas and hiking 200 miles in the deserts and forests of the American west had created some old monk cowboy mental state, a monk in China, meditating on a stone floor, staring at a wall, lived in total discomfort, a cowboy sleeping on the ground with bugs crawling on him, shivering out in the open air, hoping an Apache doesn't come in the night to kill him, also lived in total discomfort, and they could do that, because of their sincerity.

Noah lived in 2014, in a world where sincerity was addiction and addiction was sincerity.

He lived in a world where sincerity was not honored. Everyone was expected to get a self-help book and move on to the next psychological replacement.

Noah Cicero didn't know how to end the poem. If you want, you can imagine him referencing the television show *Breaking Bad* or a cicada in Japan making its shrill ring-ring noise, endlessly looking for love.

Then Noah said fuck it and said, "*And the darkness has not overcome it.*"

XXXXXX XXXXXXXXX

XXX XXXX XX
XXXXXXX XXXXXXX

XX XXX XXXX
XX XXX XXXXXX

XXXXXX XX XXXX.

XXXX XX XXXXX XX. XX
XXX XXXXXXX.

Previous poem had to be deleted because it was lies and hysteria in Noah's mind.

Okay here I go, I'm going to write this poem:

A girl had a crush on Noah, they kissed in the Grand Canyon
forest,
walked to the bottom of the canyon together,
they said sweet things to each other.
But she moved back to her country—
a country deep in Europe.

Noah went to Vegas and slowly lost his mind,
Miss Europe never stopped messaging,
telling him "I love you," "I love you," "I love you."
Noah didn't need her love, her validation.

He felt annoyed by her pleas.

He never thought of the girl in Europe,
even though she was wonderful and nice and smart,
and loved Noah for being Noah. She never
crossed his mind.

Then it hit him, that is what he was doing

to her, the woman deep in the East,
on the coast of Lake Erie.

Noah Cicero = annoying fuckhead.
He was annoying the girl in the East. She (
think about him that much, if at all some (

She didn't think about him.

He freaked out and wrote eight horrible
text messages, the meanest things
he had ever said to anyone.

She didn't respond to one. She either felt bad for him,
felt truly guilty, or just felt extremely annoyed by this
asshole she once dated.

Noah Cicero didn't mind when people died, because that is
the order of life, everything dies and changes into another
substance
and that substance changes into another substance.

But to be
rejected
then forgotten in an efficient manner.

(Noah Cicero's brain just made a huge smashing sound, like a
mountain avalanche, a guitar getting too close to the amp, a
nuclear-type scene, gore blood gnashing of teeth the ineffable
noise of truth.)

o decided months later to tell himself he didn't
.y she left him, and it was okay.)

(Sometimes he told himself that she loved him and just didn't
have the courage to say it, and in the right conditions on the
right night with the right amount of alcohol she would let him
touch her hair.)

He stopped annoying her, he has yet to bother her since.

A Missing Poem

Vendetta

Noah Cicero's life
was mostly a vast collection
of cultural appropriations.
His love of Asian food,
using chopsticks
and Asian religion.
His love for the southwest
and Native American mysticism.

But the vendetta,
the vendetta was deep
in his genetics.

He could hate
with a deep sincerity.
He could carry a grudge
for years.

After three generations
in America, the Sicilian
had almost been wiped clean

by American consumerism,
its admiration
for the Protestant work ethic
and self-help philosophy. But
the vendetta remained.

At least he did not have to
appropriate that.

The Unspeakable Truth

Noah was meditating
on his adobe porch
in Northwest Las Vegas—

When a man flew on
a cloud to him.
It was Jeon Uchi.
The Taoist magician who lives
on Mount Taebaek.

Noah was taken to North Korea—
to sit on a mat on Mount Taebaek.

Jeon gave Noah a cup of tea.

Noah asked him—
What is the most unspeakable truth.

Jeon Uchi replied, "What is an
unspeakable truth, a truth
that everyone knows, but no one

wants to hear said out loud."

Noah tried to sip his tea, but
it was too hot.

Jeon Uchi continued:
"Norman Mailer stabbed his wife,
DFW bought a gun to kill a guy,
William S. Burroughs shot
and killed his wife. Kerouac
had a daughter he paid child support for,
but refused to see. These people

were epic assholes.

People will love people
no matter what
terrible shit they do.

We forgive people, even when
they don't ask for forgiveness.

When there is no
atonement,
no penance.

Why do we love people?
Why do we forgive evil?
Stupidity—
Shallowness—
the darkest motives.

We forgive
because we are attached,
we have known them a long time,
we have put them into the
category of family or friend.
We want to have sex with them.
Because they entertain us.

We even forgive child molesters
if they make good movies.

The unspeakable truth
is that we need written laws
that have mystic origins—
with weapons to keep
them upheld.

Because we are too
forgiving of our friends
and family. We take their side,
even when we know
they are wrong, and lying.

The world would collapse
into chaos without law
not because we are
savage beasts, but because
we are so forgiving."

Noah's tea was finally
cool enough to sip.

Utilitarian Emotions

Noah Cicero had a tragic flaw.
The emotion of not
wanting to be rejected
was more important
than wanting actual love.

A Chingu in Seattle

We sat many a Saturday
on the bank of the Han River,
in Seoul. Drinking makkoli,
looking at Basquiats, talking
about what it means to be Jewish,
when we danced at Susie Q's to
"Changes" by David Bowie.

I was happy that night.

You thought David Bowie said,
"Time may change me, but
I can't change time," and you
said that was deep and awesome.
I agreed it was awesome.
Later I looked up the lyrics and it
said "trace time" and we both got angry.

When I listen to "Changes" by David Bowie,
I sing the word "change" and not "trace."

We saw each other a year later, in Seattle.
From the edge of Asia to the
edge of North America.
We like edges.

I was having a lot of problems, I couldn't stop
crying and having panic attacks. I tried
to keep it a secret. What secrets
did you have?

I sat in the hotel room you purchased,
and cried and could not get it together.

We stood in front of the Space Needle,
had someone take a picture of us
making a heart. It didn't much look like a heart,
and everyone just laughed.

You told me you were getting a doctorate
in Korea, I asked if you wanted to be a
Korean professor in America. You said,
"No, only to study."
I remembered one of my Korean students,
a 15-year-old boy who said,
"To study is the sincere way of life."

When you were leaving, you forgot your sweater.
I remembered the sweater, you bought it
after we had dinner in Hongdae. The girlfriends
we had then are gone, but we are still here.

I send a text to be honest, about your sweater
still being there. But I kind of wanted you
to forget it, so I could keep it. And sometimes
I could wear it and it would be like
I was wearing our good times in Seoul, but
you came back and took your nice sweater.

No one in the room knew what pain I was in.

There is a line from "The River Merchant's Wife"
translated by Ezra Pound.
It reads:
"The monkeys make sorrowful noise overhead."

That is how I feel.
"The monkeys make sorrowful noise overhead."

If you are coming through the southwest desert,
please let me know beforehand.
and I will come out to meet you,
as far as Phoenix.

Calling My Parents

I haven't called my parents
in three weeks.

I couldn't call them.

What was the update?

Father Mother
I have no hope.

My brother your son
also had no hope,
and he killed himself.

I have no hope, too.

I can barely function anymore,
I have to take pills
to walk from my bedroom
to the living room.

Sometimes I get enough
discipline to drive to Starbucks.

I feel no pressure to impress you,
to impress anyone anymore.

And when a person loses pressure,
he has nothing to gain. Maybe I am trying
to reach enlightenment. To be
a desert sage.

But you are from Ohio, you know
nothing of sages. You wanted me to
go to college, get a job, find a wife,
get a mortgage, there is nothing
wrong with that. I know a lot of people
who have followed that track,
and have become happy.

I am sincerely sorry,
I could not be normal.
In any way.

I know it took a lot of time,
a lot of effort,
a lot of money,
to get me grown,
and I didn't become
anything like you. I live
2,000 miles away from you.
And I don't even have a job.

I'm 33 now, I am a little old.
I don't think I can catch up,
and become a normal person.
I'm not sure if I even want to live
anymore. But I will keep living,
one suicide is enough
for a family.

Mom Gravel Driveway

When I was little,
I had a long gravel driveway
in broadleaf Ohio
in abandoned steel mill Ohio
in Chevy plant Ohio
where my mother worked.

She worked the
3 to 11 shift.

I never saw her after school,
or before school to be honest.
I made my own breakfast.
Some nights I couldn't sleep,
till her car came rolling
up the long driveway
till I heard the gravel rattle.

Till I knew she was home,
in the house with me.

Then I would fall asleep,
but now I sleep alone.
And the gravel does not rattle.

Every woman I ever loved,
is loved by another.

At 11:45pm I listen
for any car, even tires
spinning over smooth pavement.
When I hear the sound
I am looking for,
I tell myself it is you,
you are home
and I sleep.

NDE Videos on YouTube

I have been watching
a lot of Near Death Experience
videos on YouTube.

I went outside
took a walk
and tried to imagine God—
based on the NDE videos.

God seemed like an all-loving
ball of super energy thing.

I heard a philosophy prof
say once, he didn't think
there was a God because
his sister died. Seemed
really trite. If there was a super
ball of awesome energy thing
that could create universes,
seems like that Thing
would know the long-term

and understand it, and we could
not understand it, because
we are finite and consumed
with attachment and the immediate.
But the philosophy prof loved
his sister, and he needed
to hate something.

But Christians, and Muslims
Hindus and Buddhists
need someone to hate too.

Seems like the super orb
of incredible energy infinite thing
probably understands
the human hate thing.

I have actually hated
every philosophy professor
I've ever met.

There is a lesbian
sitting at the next table
at this Starbucks, she
has a bracelet that says
"fuck off" and a really bad haircut.
A black woman in her forties just
walked by, she had giant hair,
looked like she worked at a boring
middle-class job.

A guy dressed in army fatigues
is sitting at another table.

According to religious people
God can't love all three
of these different people.

But for some reason
Starbucks will serve everyone
regardless of their chosen
bullshit lifestyle, but God
has less sympathy, less empathy,
less love than Starbucks, lol
lol lol lol lol lol lol lol. Assholes.

The thing that scares people
the most about God
is that he does not discriminate.

That something could love stupid Republicans who hate
women and homos, and it loves
the stupid homos who wear "fuck off"
bracelets, and all the stupid people
in prisons with 4th grade reading levels,
all the stupid people who eat
corn-syrup-based foods, all the
stupid assholes who fight
in the military for the corporations,
and all the stupid assholes
who work at corporations,
and probably even all the stupid

assholes working at factories
in China, all the stupid assholes
in Africa who have insane notions
about how to cure AIDS. All
the stupid assholes, every
single stupid asshole
that ever lived, and this
ball of super love energy thing
might even love animals, insects, plant life,
stupid pigeons
stupid palm trees,
all the stupid people who
don't know fashion,
don't know politics,
don't know the Bible,
don't know _____
don't know _____
all the stupid
assholes who became plastic
surgeons, all the stupid asshole
cashiers at Wal-Mart.

It is really scary to think
that some super lovely
energy thing would even
take the time to love
these stupid assholes.

Need Love

According to people,
people who know things.

When you die,
you meet God,
and it feels like
love.

Like super love,
unconditional love!!!

I thought,
do I need love?
Or am I
too cool for love?

I thought about
the people who love me,
and those I love,
and how that feels,

then a small six pound cat
sat on my chest.
Then the cat
booped me.

Jesus in Wal-Mart

Noah Cicero went to Wal-Mart
to get a prescription filled.

Walking through Wal-Mart
he felt tired from the anti-anxiety pill
he took in the morning.

He did feel mildly suicidal,
not that he would kill himself, but
if a magical wind swept him away
and took him to a heaven
on the moon Europa, he would
have been happy to go.

He walked among the products.
A man with prison tats,
brown teeth and a t-shirt
with holes in it.

The man had no fashion, he probably
didn't even know what an American Apparel

even was, he couldn't handle
an OS operating system. His house
was for sure dirty, he probably hadn't
washed around the bathtub, ever.

He said, "Hey."
Noah looked over. "Me?"
"Yeah you, Jesus told me
you need help."
Noah said nothing.
The man tried putting his arm
around Noah, but Noah said
in a nervous voice, "Please
don't touch me."

The man with the brown teeth
said, "It isn't that bad, it'll get better soon."

Noah responded,
"This is so horrible,
it doesn't even seem real."

The man with the brown teeth
looked into Noah's eyes and said,
"It'll be okay."

Noah wanted to scream,
"But the pain is in my brain,
and I can't escape
my own brain."

The man went away,
walked back
to whatever filthy apartment he lived in.

Noah Cicero sat in his car,
with eyes so sad, he said,
"Am I really that sad?" He remembered
everyone who tried to help him
in the last six months, Bernice, John, Wanda,
Nicky, Sara, Haley, Cameron, Keegan, Mani,
Paulina, Asia, Dana, Samantha, etc., etc.

But nothing worked—
Noah was so fucked—
that Jesus personally had to send a guy
with brown teeth to notify him
the depression must end.

He put both hands on his temples,
and said, "Please stop,
please stop please stop
the noise."

Han Shan Gets a Job on Cold Mountain

"Can't you get a job using your degree"
"I'm sure you'll get a job by the end
of next week"
"Have you tried Indeed.com"
"Have you tried convenience stores"
"Have you tried job fairs"
"Have you tried Facebook"
"Have you tried watching YouTube
tutorials on how to get a job"

Noah looks up and points at them—
pokes them in the chest—
God made me a poet—
God made Han Shan a poet,
He put Han Shan on Cold Mountain,
and he put me in this desert.

I've never asked any of you
to stop making money
to work less hard

For me to write
of Cold Mountain.
I must live there,
at all times.

On the summit, in the caves,
sleeping under the bristlecone pines,
because you can't live
on Cold Mountain.
You have better things to do.

My job is to bring you water
from the melted snow
that makes its streams,
so when you need Cold Mountain
I'll be there
to provide you with water.

But for right now,
leave me the fuck alone!
I'm on Cold Mountain
and I'll come down
when *the wind* tells me to,
not because of
an ad on Craigslist!

Tina Turner

You know that noise
Tina Turner makes
before she sings the chorus
of "What's Love Got to Do With It"

I am that noise.

Starbucks Pigeon

A pigeon running through
the Starbucks parking lot.

A small child walks over
and scares the pigeon.

EBT Dreams

My woman left me, but it has been
so long I can't even complain anymore.
I tell myself because of her,
I am in the Las Vegas Welfare Office.

She is my favorite scapegoat. Take
an anti-anxiety pill and calm down, Noah.

The line starts at the door, I wait in line
for an hour, blacks, whites, Mexicans,
and even a few Asians. We all need
food, WICK or ObamaCare.

I need food. Desert poet has no food.

Everyone discusses
the death of the Ultimate Warrior,
a famous wrestler from the 90s.

I said I remembered seeing him wrestle
when I was a little kid. A black guy my age

said, "Yeah, we all remember."

If the Ultimate Warrior is dead,
we all must die. Because he was
THE ULTIMATE.

The definition of ULTIMATE:
"the best achievable or imaginable of its kind."

There is no music in the Welfare Office,
no pictures on the wall, only gray.

Two overweight security guards
making less than ten dollars an hour
yell at poor people all day
to stay in line, to wait their turn,
they took my coffee, there is a
no food and drink rule.

I finally get through the line,
then they tell me to sit, they will
call me to go to a room to meet
with a caseworker.

I sit in a chair next to
an old Mexican man
wearing a jogging suit
with a freshly shaved head.

Remembered my grandparents,
all of them died comfortable,

they never had to wear jogging suits
or go to welfare offices,
of course they were white.

The black people and Mexicans
don't like seeing me in the Welfare Office.
If a white man with blue eyes
can't get a job, what chance do they have?

After two hours I meet with a caseworker,
tired white woman, mid 30s. Dealing with
frustrated angry semi-crazy hungry poor people all day.
I said, "Did you hear the Ultimate Warrior died?"
She responded, "Did you know
the Ultimate Warrior could only breathe
the air of combat?"
She gets me an EBT card.
$189 party time!

Eight Horrible Text Messages

Noah Cicero sent
the eight most horrible
text messages,
total cruelty,
hate mania!!!

To someone
who saved him, who for several years
made his life very interesting.

He had gratitude.
He told himself
he had to write the eight horrible texts.
It was the only way to ensure
there would never be contact again.

Why couldn't he walk away peacefully?
Just be happy that he got to travel
the world with a beautiful woman,
be happy that a girl seven years younger
let him sleep with her, and on some days

even loved him.

After Noah Cicero wrote the horrible
text messages, the woman he wrote them to
began to disappear from his mind every day.
Noah's family said, "It had to be done."

blood had to be shed

Noah put the pictures away, he even
took the cute note she wrote from
the first year of their relationship
out of his wallet, he couldn't throw it away,
no one expected him to.

He used to dream of a Murakami ending,
but now, even that was destroyed.

He took all the memories of her except one,
he considered all the other memories excess,
he threw the surplus memories away,
even the memories of when they first met,
he put them aside.

He focused now on a neutral memory,
of her standing at Angkor Wat in Cambodia,
in her blue jean dress, wearing her Marc Jacobs sunglasses,
they walked the walls touching the carvings,
together they watched a monkey drink from a bottle of water.
They had never seen a wild monkey before.

Of course he will love again,
of course he will accomplish more things,
of course he will grow old,
when no one is paying attention
he will say, "Wasn't Cambodia beautiful?"
and she will say, "Yeah, I liked the happy pizza."

And of course Noah Cicero will grow old and die,
and of course she will grow old and die.

The Old Woman's Mind

There is a zen koan,
it goes
A student asked a zen master,
"I haven't anything in my mind,
what should I do?"
Master said, "Throw it out."
"But I haven't anything in it."
Master said, "Then carry it out."

An old woman lived with Noah Cicero,
she wasn't that old, she was only 63,
but she was dying of cirrhosis,
and looked 75.
She sat in the other room playing
on Facebook. She hardly ever
left her room, she had stopped cleaning,
stopped cooking meals, she barely ever
stood up, since 1987.

They took her two foster kids then,
then her mother died in 1993, then her father in 2002,

then her husband in 2013.

She moved so little, her body
had atrophied. She only ate enriched white bread
and canned food.

Noah would check on her several times a day,
"Are you okay?"
She would start talking about something from
1985. The memory was vivid, and when he told
her daughter of the memory, her daughter
said that memory wasn't even remotely accurate.

Even though she just looked
like a dying old woman,
there was a world in her mind she had constructed
to tolerate existence.

The old woman didn't know
she demanded everyone treat her
like a princess. Others had to do her shopping,
others had to clean up after her, others
had to drive her around.

As soon as we left her alone,
she went back
to a world where everyone was alive,
where her foster children were small.

In a movie starring Julia Roberts
or Jennifer Lawrence, the sad character

would decide in a perfect epiphany
that she needed to 'carry it out'
and get on with life.

But sometimes, it doesn't happen.
Sometimes
there is no redemption.

Two Happy Places

1.

The Buddha
holds up a flower
the audience stares
Mahākāśyapa learns
the ineffable wisdom.

2.

Monkey fights The Buddha.
The Buddha holds out his palm.
Says, "Jump over my palm."
Monkey jumps miles into heaven's sky,
makes a mark on the ground.
Monkey looks up and sees Buddha.
Buddha says, "Look down."
The mark Monkey made is
only on Buddha's thumb.
Then Buddha says,
"You could not even
jump over my thumb."

So Many Drinks

He told her as they walked
down the strip,
in the lights of the Bellagio,
"I drank myself to sleep
for four months straight,
it was just
part of everything."

She responded,
"I drank every day
from age 22 to 28."
Then she smiled.

March 22nd, 2014

Noah Cicero woke up in Las Vegas to the worst feeling he had ever had, the suicide feeling. He had never seen this feeling before, it had complete control. He couldn't move. He just wanted his mind to stop thinking about her, running the same stupid infomation over and over again in his head. Then a blast went off in his mind, Noah Cicero was his six-year-old self, a little version of Noah Cicero.

The room was nothing but whitespace. Even the chair six-year-old Noah Cicero was sitting on was white.

The little boy was crying, head down.

There was nothing left to grasp, the wind had taken it all away.

Noah Cicero had nothing left, he fought and fought, greedy to make reality work the way he wanted. And none of it worked.

No one left to blame.

No one to be angry at.

His six-year-old self sat there crying.

Then he heard someone yell, "Brother!"

Little Noah Cicero looked up and saw a young 1980s Hulk Hogan, wearing his red Hulkamaniac head band, his yellow shirt to soon be ripped off, and his red underwear thing. Noah Cicero's mind searched and searched, looking for anything, for one true belief that remotely seemed true and beautiful. And this is what his mind found.

Hulk Hogan yelled at the crying boy, "Are you a Hulkamaniac?"

"Yes," he said, whimpering.

"Hulkamaniacs don't kill themselves, brother. Remember when I bodyslammed Andre the Giant!!! Everyone said I couldn't do it, everyone said it was impossible!!! But I charged up, I took the energy from all the Hulkamaniacs. Through the power of all the Hulkamaniacs I was able to bodyslam the 500-pound Andre the Giant!!!"

The little boy looked up at the Hulk, the Hulk danced around, flexing his muscles, screaming, giving it everything he had to keep Noah Cicero alive.

"Hulkamaniacs don't kill themselves because I need the energy of every little Hulkster to keep me strong, to give me the energy to bodyslam my opponents into the ground!!!"

Then the Hulk began shaking and sucking in the energy of all the Hulkamaniacs. The energy swirled around in him like a wind, the power of a million Hulkamaniacs.

Then Hogan screamed, "24-inch pythons!!!"

Then the Hulk put his giant hands on the shoulders of the boy, made him stand up, and said, "Brother, I'll show you how to gather energy." Hulk Hogan began shaking violently, flexing his muscles, whipping his head back and forth. The boy felt scared but he started shaking, flexing his muscles and whipping his head. He felt the power of Hulkamania surge through him. It was there, the power, the power that surged through the strong unstoppable body that was Hulk Hogan.

Then the Hulk got down real low and yelled, "Get on the biggest back in the world and I'll carry you." The little boy had stopped crying. His face changed to a smile. He jumped on the Hulk's back, the biggest back in the world. 33-year-old Noah Cicero stood up, took a shower, brushed his teeth, washed his hair and when he saw his sister later in the day, he told his sister a funny cliche, because sometimes all we have is cliches. "Today is the first day of the rest of my life," and his sister responded, "Thank god."

George Jones 2

I sat close
to a woman,
an educated woman,
like me she had traveled Asia—
Japan China Cambodia India Korea.

We had both seen Angkor Wat

An impressive person,
on the Las Vegas strip
we talked of seeing Buddhist monks,
and riding metro subways
but my heart
would not work—
I knew I was over her,
but not *it*.

The impressive woman
confessed she had been to
Asia, with another.

The man she had traveled with
was gone, she did not speak his name.
For her also
only the *it* remained.

Is this how you become a cowboy?

We both went home alone that night.

George Jones 3

I saw on your twitter
that you want revenge
that you have a vendetta against me—

For the eight horrible texts
I sent

But can't you see—
you don't need to do anything
to get revenge

Every time you say anything funny
or laugh

And I'm not there to hear it
you get revenge
you win

and now
that you give your jokes and giggles to another

(Noah Cicero couldn't finish the poem,
there was a blue sky, not one cloud,
and it was a little chilly in Las Vegas
that day. He lay back in his chair
on the patio of the Lake Mead Starbucks.
He put on George Jones.
He folded his arms and stared
at the peaks of the Spring Mountains.)

Then he wrote
"I am powerless"

He reached down in his REI satchel
and took his second anti-anxiety pill
of the morning.

Cowboy Koans

1.

The student is drinking water
from a plastic bottle.

Student says, "What is zen?"
to the master.

Master says, "Can you drink
the word water?"

Student looks
at his bottle of water.

Student says, "Whoa."

2.

Student said, "I really
considered suicide."

Master said,
"You don't have to kill yourself,
it is already over."

3.

Master: What is a hammer?

Student 1: It is shaped like a T and made of metal.

Student 2: It puts nails into walls.

Master: *(pointing at wall)* The feeling you get from that picture.

Stupid Ex-Boyfriend Writes Bad Poem

Also Known As:

(The Fashion Dream Failed)

(Toaster Strudel Rom Com)

(Makkoli on The Han)

(Stevie Nicks 1976 Singing Rhiannon live on a show called *Midnight Express*)

(Stevie Nicks is the music, Stevie Nicks became the Old Welsh Witch)

(A Small Gray Cat Knocks Things Off the Table, Wakes us Up)

(A Small Gray Excessively Furry Cat)

(Yeah, Our Relationship was a Non Sequitur)

(Annoying Ex-Boyfriend Annoys Annoys Annoys)

(Bon Iver's Skinny Love)

1.

Agency!!!
I won't take your agency away anymore.

I won't do anything to/for/with you anymore
and you won't
do anything to/for/with me anymore

an absolute silence
between us

2.

I should say thank you—
You taught me how to be cool,
you taught me how to wear clothes that fit.

I put down the black hoody
and baggy blue jeans.

Now I wear Japanese jeggings
and American Apparel.

You actually made me really happy
and sometimes you were tender.

Your most tender moment was during
the taxi rides home from Hongdae.
A long 45 minute ride drunk at 5am.

I always fell asleep, you would
hold me like I was a baby, so sweet.

But then you would wake me up in Gunpo,
because you were afraid of speaking Korean,
to say, "여기, 여기"

I thought I had Stevie Nicks,
1976 Stevie Nicks
tenderness mixed with drugs
and early morning bloody marys.
my own Stevie,
my own gypsy.

I looked at Stevie Nicks' Wiki page,
Stevie Nicks sleeps alone at night.

3.

Not even
Sailor Moon
could save our relationship

Moon crisis

4.

We met at a coffee shop
in southeast Portland

lightly snowing

I sat with Lisa.
Mutual friend
on her couch
she handed me organic tea—

Remember we did a video
on Adderall
Lisa kept smoking weed
it was funny

Lisa asks,
"What do you have?"

"A Martin guitar."

"Must be freeing to have nothing."

"The things I wanted I didn't own."

5.

I preferred when you cuddled me
your little gymnast arm
slightly furry
holding me firmly

I would hold your bicep
with my left hand.

6.

The idea you exist.
It isn't an idea.
You factually exist.

That you exist somewhere
going to work, doing the dishes,
doing yoga, probably even smiling at times,

And I have to pretend you don't exist

Seems odd.

The idea
of you being happy
mildly
pisses me off

I am a white man

with blue eyes
even a little fit
books published
college degree
GPA 3.3

What gave you the right
to leave me?
What kangaroo court
did you find?
That granted the ruling
to leave me?

7.

I think our song
was "Home" by
Edward Sharpe
and the Magnetic Zeros

You sang it to me
shirtless
in B's apartment
at that highly
sexualized/politicized party.

I always told myself
it was "Home."
But if you were asked,
you would probably laugh

and not have an answer—

8.

On Sundays
On warm days
we would go to Seoul.

You always loved crossing the river by subway.

I loved it too.

Bought a bottle of makkoli,
filled our little paper cups,
sat by the river.

Someone jumped off the Mapo Bridge once,
we watched policemen
on boats
with long hooks
fish for a human body—

We didn't feel compassion
but interest as foreigners
seeing Korean suicide rituals

9.

I am on so much medication

now
I don't even know
if you ever loved me

or if I ever loved you

or if we ever loved each other.

10.

Noah Cicero tried to analyze
what is The Pain he feels

The Pain that caused all the panic attacks

and fear

and the inability to see any options

The Pain that closed off
the future
and now.

Noah Cicero said to a lizard
in the desert.

The lizard scurried,
then rested by a cactus.

"Do I still love her?

or am I afraid
to want anything.
Is that enlightenment?

To tell oneself,
the world is on fire,
to want the world,
will only lead to getting burnt.

Or am I just being a wimp,
and the suffering is fun
just as much fun as the fun?"

A wind flooded the desert,
nothing moved
the desert plants and animals
were strong enough
to handle the wind.

11.

But what is
The Pain?

That you are gone?
That you left me without asking?
A genetic problem that has nothing to do with you?
That I did this to myself and view The Pain as pleasurable?
Because of childhood experiences?

I do not have enough data
to answer
but the answer isn't required

Can't pay the bills with answers

12.

I fell in love with you
during penetration

Haven't had sex in eleven months,
you were the last person I had sex with.

I have this belief if I don't have sex
for a year
I will be like a virgin again.

I tried to have sex at the six month point—
But my brain saw you—
and my penis became limp.

Seems really fucking stupid, Noah.

13.

Since September,
when we shared a bed.
I've changed a lot.

I exercise now,
stopped smoking,
stand straight up,
stopped listening to stupid political shows
on YouTube.
Now instead of debating philosophy
and politics, and then eventually
becoming a loud embarrassing dick

I talk about zen, reincarnation, and even shamans—
probably because I can't hack reality anymore.

If we speak to each other,
we turn into our dead selves—
the overgrown ruins of ourselves.

Since I am a writer, fans
will visit my wrecked ruins.
And they ask me, "Noah
come with us."

And I say now,
"Oh you can go,
I don't even know the path anymore,
I will stay here
among the casinos and palm trees."

My fans returned
and I ask,
"How was it there?"

They replied,
"Beautiful."

14.

You aren't even a real person
anymore.

A mythology?

I have made you into
a vicious tribe of Apaches.

They have me trapped,
but I have the high ground,
and I kill all the Apaches,
one by one,
myth by myth,
dream by dream
Murakami by Murakami

There was blood everywhere,
after I walked away with a limp.

15.

I will not lie
sometimes I see

a pack of Sour Patches

and
I
want to
scream

16.

When I watched you leave
at the Incheon Airport

I knew you were gone.

You wrote one last text.
"I love you peanut."

I stared at it.

We would no longer
eat pizza together,
cuddle and watch RuPaul's *Drag Race*.

It was all over.

See, I have mommy issues,
and to live in a bubble with a woman
is heaven.

When I got back to my room

in Seongnam.
After a two hour subway ride,
I started screaming,
"Where is S"
"Where is S"
"Where is S"

I took your shoes,
and put them nicely by the door.
Put your clothes on hangers.

And just stared
at them

and cried.

17.

When you dropped
me off at the Akron Airport
two months later,
to work at the Grand Canyon

I saw you crying.

18.

When I came back
from the Grand Canyon

for two weeks,
I spent the night at your apartment,
but I could tell
you had already moved on.

The last time I saw you.

You dropped me off
at my parents.

We had spaghetti dinner,
and my dad made me wash your car.

(At this moment go on YouTube and put on Bon Iver's "Skinny
Love." Noah Cicero prefers the live version he did on a British
TV show. Play it over and over again.)

We hugged.

And you drove away.

Every muscle hurts in my body,
thinking about that moment.

19.

It gets harder and harder
to write these lines.

The inspiration is being blown out.

Busy with life again, new jobs, new goals,
even new friends.

Not one ember left,
just charred wood.

Now we may forget each other.

(Noah Cicero has been staring blankly listening to "Skinny Love"
for twenty minutes in the Mojave Desert in the patio area of a
Starbucks with his arms folded, trying not to cry. He types one
last line. Then listens to "Skinny Love" for another twenty minutes
before going home.)

You are still the prettiest girl in the world.

Tweets from a Mexican Family Dollar Employee Who Has Three Followers on Twitter

my ex has turned into Scanner Darkly

the only thing I have to do is stay alive till I'm dead

i just told someone there is a Walgreens next to a Jack in the Box

i invented something called 'tanning meditation'

started to believe that working retail might be poverty heaven

i stopped justifying

nothing is happening I like it

there is nothing to fear but the mental state of frustration and anger

i keep telling my own thoughts to "shut the fuck up"

this is my face

i have an idea of myself now if i speak to you a dead version idea of myself appears to kill the new version idea of myself can't let that happen lo siento lol

you are really bad for yourself

i wanted to watch a movie but forgot how

standing next to plant, oh wow i'm a person

because of you, i brush my teeth every night

i don't believe you

i don't think about those things

you aren't even that person anymore

I am really pretty and intelligent, why are people torturing me

if you eat Indian buffet and hike with me, i'll love you forever

wish people worried about their sense of humors as much as their bodies

i brush my teeth every night

people are programmed to be in love

the day you realize all your exes are pretty great and it is you that sucks

a form of zen castration

all the sentient douche bags

I am done being myself

I would like a retraction on myself

I have internalized that everything is horrible, but I won't resist
it, trying to resist is where the pain comes from

the saddest thing is that I don't think you have ever done
anything 'embarrassing'

Now when i think about you, it is different, i don't feel bad
emotions, i imagine seeing you again in some weird place, my
face hardened a little by the desert sun, and you're like i don't
know

everyone is really creepy, so fucking creepy

what if enlightenment is internalizing how lame everyone/
everything is

everyone is inside everything, but everything is not everyone

lol

I have started wearing deodorant, it doesn't contain aluminum

people are outnumbered by things that are not people

I didn't write this to make you feel guilty or embarrass you

the only weapon i have is silence

i don't hate you

the longer we're apart, the more we change into different people

the Seoul subway map

I'll meet you in 문산

I'll meet you at the water tower

Looking back on it, you did try to become friends and say you were sorry. Shit

I don't smoke and have psoriasis anymore and I stand straight up.

You followed me on Twitter, took a pic of it on my iPhone, i have evidence. you unfollowed me 16 hours later

Sometimes, not often, but sometimes I play "Band of Gold" by Freda Payne and wait for knocks at the door (I imagine you buying plane tickets alone in your bed in Cleveland, having our mutual friend drive you to the airport, our mutual friend saying in her grand style, "gotta do what you gotta do." You sitting in a plane seat biting your nails, popping Xanax. Spending your last dollars to rent a car)

there are no knocks

My funnest days are behind me, but my most glorious days are ahead.

To those who saved me: I will show up at your calling hours unannounced and give a testimony on how you once saved a man.

Oma Bernice Mullins, Wanda Mullins, John Talkington, Sara Childers, Hayley Anderson, Samantha Ditomaso, Cameron Pierce, Sam Pink, Lily Hoang, Jordan Castro, Rachel and Rebeccah Hershkovits, Dana Killmeyer, Nicholas Chiarella, James Chapman, ZK Lowenfels, Madison Langston, Jake Levine and Fin Dog.

CPSIA information can be obtained
at www.ICGtesting.com
Printed in the USA
BVHW070239110419
545236BV00002B/397/P